Ten Fat Sausages

illustrated by Elke Zinsmeister

Child's Play (International) Ltd

dney
hina

Ten fat sausages sizzling in the pan.

One went Pop! and the other went Bang!

2

Eight fat sausages sizzling in the pan.

One went Pop! and the other went Bang!

Four fat sausages sizzling in the pan.

One went Pop! and the other went Bang!

10

o fat sausages sizzling in the pan.

8 6 4 2 0

one went Pop! and none went Bang!